Lucy Jesup

Extracts from the Papers and Letters

SALZWASSER
VERLAG

Lucy Jesup

Extracts from the Papers and Letters

Reprint of the original, first published in 1858.

1st Edition 2023 | ISBN: 978-3-37514-942-0

Verlag (Publisher): Salzwasser Verlag GmbH, Zeilweg 44, 60439 Frankfurt, Deutschland
Vertretungsberechtigt (Authorized to represent): E. Roepke, Zeilweg 44, 60439 Frankfurt, Deutschland
Druck (Print): Books on Demand GmbH, In de Tarpen 42, 22848 Norderstedt, Deutschland

EXTRACTS

FROM THE

PAPERS AND LETTERS

OF

LUCY JESUP.

SUDBURY:

PUBLISHED BY WRIGHT AND GILBERT, MARKET HILL.

LONDON: A. W. BENNETT, BISHOPSGATE STREET.

1858.

It is believed that the following pages will be acceptable to those who were more or less acquainted with the writer; while it may prove interesting to some others to peruse these few records of the mental exercises of one who had long been a subject of the "chastening," which to nature is indeed "not joyous, but grievous;" unknown as these were to most but by the evidence of "the peaceable fruits of righteousness" in a life and conversation influenced by the power of divine grace.

EXTRACTS,

&c.

LUCY JESUP, daughter of Samuel and Mary Jesup, of Halstead, was born on the 26th of 6th month, 1807. In her earliest years a warmth of temper was apparent, which required the exercise of kind and judicious maternal care; this it was her privilege to share, and under its influence, through the divine blessing, her lively disposition ripened into a sweetness of character which endeared her to her youthful associates. Before attaining her twentieth year a delicacy of constitution became apparent. Several times she was for months together confined to a recumbent position, and she never recovered her former state of health. Thus deprived of ability for pursuing the usual active engagements of life, and prevented from mingling in general society, she was still enabled to minister by kind attentions to her beloved parents in their declining years, to add to the comfort of remaining relatives, and to enjoy a degree of personal and epistolary intercourse with her friends,—one of whom thus writes :

"It is perhaps difficult for those who were intimately acquainted with dear L. J. in her mature age and during her secluded life, to give a clear idea of her character without indulging in too much expression of individual feeling; yet it may not be undesirable to say that there was a loveliness of mind in various respects, attractive and endearing to those who enjoyed her friendship, and that this was felt by them as an influence for good. She

B

possessed a peculiar warmth of attachment towards her friends, and evinced a tender sympathy in their sorrows. Her affectionate letters often conveyed a word of consolation to the sad or suffering, as well as an animated participation in the joys and comforts of those whom she addressed. Her love of nature was remarkably strong, so that, even when confined to a sick room, a present of flowers, a gleam of sunset, or the distant note of some well-known bird, was hailed with delight. Yet it has been remarked of her, that in times of comparative health, the solemn truth that this is not our rest, was ever borne in mind, and stamped upon her remaining earthly joys.

" Thus was apparent, in some measure, the blessed fruit of afflictions dispensed, in the loss of many beloved relatives and her own long-continued weakness ; these were, it is believed, sanctified in her experience, and led to the carrying into effect the exhortation ' Set your affections on things above.' Yet was not her invalid state exempt from hidden trials and temptations as regarded the things of earth,—' the work of the enemy,' she would say, ' to spoil the purity of our enjoyments.' In these conflicts she felt the victory was with her Saviour alone, and to Him she carried her sorrows and looked for saving strength."

"When able to read or listen, works of instruction or general information were a source of pleasure and interest, especially the memoirs and letters of religious persons ; dear L. had also a strong relish for poetry, but was led carefully to avoid what could not profit, and (especially of later times) found it best to abstain from fiction entirely, doubtless perceiving that this kind of mental food did not prove salutary to spiritual life and health."

" One other token of the regulating power of Divine love was a scrupulous care to refrain from speaking ill of the absent ; the erring being almost invariably mentioned, (if at all) in words of pity rather than of blame. These things may be worthy of notice, as evidences that the work of grace was making progress in the soul, and suggest a searching of heart, as to whether a similar ' carefulness,' and ' clearing of themselves' is wrought in those who survive, that they may, through redeeming mercy, in hours of trial and at the end of time, experience that peace, and that stedfast hope, which was the portion of their departed friend."

The following memorandum is without date, but it appears to refer to the time when those which immediately follow it were written.

" Although the visitations of Divine Love to my soul had been at seasons mercifully extended, (yet alas, how often slighted) it was not, I think till early in the year 1828 that the way of salvation was clearly manifested; not till then that I was enlightened to 'behold the Lamb of God which taketh away the sin of the world;' having faith afforded to believe in Him as my Saviour and Redeemer, to whom I was strengthened to apply ' for grace to pardon all my sin,' and to trust in Him as the only Mediator between God and man. It pleased my Heavenly Father by a dream to instruct me; I thought I had to contend with a powerful army; it was in array against me, and I believed death to be inevitable, as I was not under the protection of any one, but I saw a person who I was assured would intercede for me, so that there would be no fear of death. I felt soon perfectly at ease, and awoke under the consciousness that it was the Saviour whom I had seen, and the conflicts of mind I had had to pass through in previous waking hours were permitted to subside, giving place to a humble faith in the Captain of our Salvation. The middle wall of partition between God and my soul seemed in mercy broken down."

"5th month, 1828. The last week has been to me a
fast; I seem wandering in search of something to sustain
me, but I can find nothing; I seem dead to all that is
good, and to have lost ability to seek after it ; I feel as if
I could enjoy nothing until I taste of that food which
comes from Heaven; how weak I am when left alone!
I believe that negligence in seeking for true sustenance
has brought me into this wilderness, this solitary place;
oh when will it rejoice and blossom as the rose? not
until my Heavenly Father makes me glad, and removes
from my heart a weight of iniquity. Oh, that I were
more diligent in waiting at the footstool of my Redeemer;
that my faith and love were made perfect in Him, that I
were willing to be stripped of every false covering! when
will the day dawn and the day star arise in my heart?
Left to myself I must perish, but surely Jesus is 'the
crown of my hope,' 'his grace is sufficient for me,' but I
must seek after it with more earnestness. May I be
helped to do so."

" 5th month, 16th. Since writing the above I have
been favoured with some degree of faith and confidence.
I have been made to cast myself at the feet of my dear
Redeemer, feeling that of myself I could do nothing.
What a mercy! I have also been greatly refreshed and
comforted by a visit from J. B. and B. S. to our meeting;
a feeling of heavenly peace and serenity has been granted
me, and renewed desires to give up my whole heart to
Him to whom alone it belongs. All praise is due to my
merciful Heavenly Father, and all the glory is his alone
for thus continuing to visit me with the Day-spring from
on high."

" In the 5th month, 1828, my dear sister Sarah
Knight finished her earthly course; it was to me a season
of renewed favour and deep instruction. My young heart
was made sensible of the precious and heavenly calm

which was permitted her at times, when fast sinking away."

The next memorandum in order of time is a record of feeling on the loss of her beloved sister Priscilla.

"9th month 28th, 1829. While sitting on the sofa by the side of dear Priscilla's bed a sweet calm was permitted to overspread my mind, and 'quietness covered it as a canopy;' to this feeling I had been very much a stranger, both in the sick room and out of it, yet there were seasons granted in which I was enabled calmly to trust,—and oh how thankful ought I to be that Divine support was so extended,—that I felt willing to resign this dear object of our love, who seemed in humble hope and confidence to be only waiting to be received into the arms of her Redeemer. On the 29th the solemn close took place. On that morning the dear girl was so like herself, her countenance, so *sweetly, beautifully* calm and happy, seems in memory to be present with me. Yes, dearest girl, thou looked 'all beautiful within,' while thy worn out frame would last but a few hours longer. Divine support was so mercifully near us that we could not weep, but were permitted to participate in thy fulness of joy. We found that 'in quietness and in confidence' there was strength, that it was 'The Lord's doing and marvellous in our eyes."

" In the afternoon, after having given me some little directions with the greatest composure and sweetness, thy breath became shorter, and great exhaustion after the exertion of so much whispering, indicated the approach of dissolution. Oh! how the arm of Divine support sustained and upheld me above the feelings of nature when I saw that death would soon deprive us of thee— that thou wouldst close thine eyes upon us for ever in this world. But 'with God all things are possible,' and in thy state of suffering and preparation thou didst earnestly look for the time when thou wouldst be for ever in the presence of Him whom thou desired to serve. For about half an hour before thy ransomed spirit was released, a peaceful calm—a heavenly silence, over-shadowed us. I felt it to my great support, and I thought that I partook with thee, dear girl, in this feeling, and for some days this union appeared to exist. How sweet and precious it seemed that there was a cord which death could not divide. Next morning the feelings of nature broke heavily upon me; I had but one dear sister left, yet, when I beheld thy dear remains (looking so heavenly sweet), not many tears were shed, for I felt that thou wast in the enjoyment of all thou hadst desired—that 'thy conflict was ended, the victory won.' Oh, how this cup of grief has been made comparatively palatable! It is of Divine mercy and condescension.

"In the afternoon, while sitting with dear Martha, after reading some of dear P.'s remarks relating to the state of her mind, how did I shed tears of joy on her account, and I was enabled so to realize her state of happiness, that gratitude and adoration seemed to be the clothing of my poor mind. Then the remembrance of her sufferings was taken away, and a sweet acknowledgment arose that they were nothing, compared to the enjoyment of every spiritual delight.

"On First day, the 4th of 10th month, which was one I hope never to forget, when the dear relics were con-signed to dust, I experienced such an evidence of the tender compassion of the Highest towards his poor, weak, afflicted creatures, that I should be glad if on this paper I could fully portray his mercy, that I might be able to recur to it for my own instruction. Just as I was called to follow the precious remains, I think I never felt such agonizing grief. Oh, if it had not been for that merciful and unspeakable kindness which a tender Father administered, I could not have supported it, without being really ill. My strength was gone, so that I was obliged to walk between two persons, and then could hardly get to the chaise. When the coffin was placed I sobbed aloud; I felt no comfort, no support; but when the meeting was more gathered, my tears were changed as in an instant to *tears of joy*, under the feeling that my dear sister was in the enjoyment of perfect happiness,—and truly

'He who stills the boisterous wave
Assuaged my woe.'

He brought a precious calm over my spirit, which was permitted to continue the whole of the meeting, so that at the close of it, when the coffin was removed, I could not shed a tear. Oh, what a change! What a mercy, to feel the power of Divine Love cover our spirits, and may I ever be willing to acknowledge its supreme excellency—its entire efficacy, and when I peruse this sheet may my heart expand in gratitude and adoration for this extension of Divine pity and regard. Oh, it was to me wonderful. The precious feeling of heavenly serenity lasted through this memorable day, and for some time after it was so extended at times, as to make our loss hardly felt, so that I could (instead of looking at this and the other thing which reminded me of the dear departed and weeping over them) enjoy the feeling of Divine goodness."

1st month 7th, 1830. Several names are recorded of "those among the circle of our friends who within the last few years have passed from time to eternity."

" The loss of so many, especially that of dear Priscilla, makes me feel at times very mournful. May I remember that

'His that single eye should be,
Who but trusts in Christ alone;
Trusting through His power to see,
Truths discerned not by his own!'

Even after so many trials, and in my state of debility,

some thirst for human approbation I find on reflection
yet remains, which sorrowfully proves that I still love the
world and that I am not entirely willing to give up all for
Christ.   Now I am very much secluded, and in dear
Martha's room.   I felt a little pang the other evening
when a friend called upon us who, in the days of my
strength and freedom from trial, caused me to feel, at
times, too well satisfied with that which can never really
satisfy.   Ah, the world has a cord still about my heart;
Oh, when shall I go free ? When shall I count all things
but loss, so that I may but be a poor despised follower of
a crucified Lord ; If all these trials do not accomplish
this, what will become of me ?"

"4th month, 29th.   Friends have to day been attend-
ing a funeral in our burial ground.   The recollection of
the last interment there caused nature to feel deeply.
But how much has my poor thirsty soul been refreshed
this afternoon by partaking once again of a little sustaining nourishment, which was indeed sweet to my taste, and
animating and strengthening in its effects.   Oh ! one
drop of living water does such great things, and how did
I feel again the transcendent preciousness of the extension of a little heavenly good,—of an unearthly peace
and serenity; even though it may last for a very short
season, how it lifts the soul above the trials of the world,
and ' smiles upon its storms.'   To have experienced such
a favour is indescribably sweet, after a long time of rest-
lessness and disquietude, without a sense of divine support, which I think I must attribute to a careless, easy,
indifferent state of mind.   Oh, could I go steadily on my
way looking more earnestly and habitually to ' the Strong
for strength !' The reverse of doing so has brought me
into many a trouble and perplexity, and I go along weak,
feeble and faithless."

" 5th month, 1830. I cannot feel comfortable to let the last seven months pass without further record ; it has been a time which it would be well for me to refer to more fully than by memory. Till within the last month I have been prevented by bodily indisposition and the cold weather from retiring daily to seek for a renewal of strength. It seemed as though my spiritual health was on the decline, and my desires had lost much of their fervour. Thus every Christian grace for a long season seemed to flag, and I was in danger of losing a lively sense of the excellency of a life devoted to the service of Him who has done so much for us. At the time my dear Priscilla was called from this state of existence I was in poor health, and the bereavement weighed so heavily upon me that the little strength I then had diminished very fast. I took a severe cold, attended by a bad cough, and yet to so little good effect did the death of one so beloved impress my mind, that I remember thinking ' I should be comparatively thoughtless if it were not for this cough,' which indeed appeared to me not unlikely to terminate in consumption. Yet there were other times when I felt so peaceful and happy as almost to rejoice in the hope of soon leaving this poor world, and meeting again the dear one whose loss I often deeply mourned. Very varied have been my feelings during my long confinement in dear Martha's room ; every thing in this life has often appeared gloomy, and the spiritual life at such times has frequently been at so low an ebb that I could derive nothing therefrom to cheer my dreary way. At other seasons there has been an earnest craving of spirit to bear all patiently, and to be willing to endure the variety of chastisements which sometimes I could humbly and thankfully accept as evidence of the continued love of my Heavenly Father. I have, indeed, had humiliating proofs of the unregenerate state of my heart from the lack

of submission and Christian resignation, when all without
seemed "waste and dreary;" but this experience proves
that my debt of gratitude is the greater in that the rod
has again been lifted up to correct my erring soul. Many
have been my outward trials, for which I now feel as if I
could be thankful; and many have been my inward conflicts, one in particular on the most important of all
subjects—death. The recollection of my dear sister's sufferings has been at times most distressing and over-
whelming, and how have I shuddered at the thought of
experiencing the same conflict! I felt all that nature
must when no superior power is near. But soon my fears
were silenced; the dear Redeemer, (as I lay upon my bed
one morning) was graciously pleased to reveal himself as
the entire conqueror of our last enemy, and I felt indeed
that it was in Him to rob the grave of victory, and take
the sting from death. How comforted I felt in the full
trust and persuasion that my dear Priscilla was borne in
His arms through the dark valley, and through his mercy
and unmerited love safely landed for ever. Then my
fearful anxious heart was melted in gratitude, and tears
of joy were shed in consideration of such boundless love.

 "About two months since, I raised a little blood, which
produced much agitation and alarm; I could not feel
composed, but all was fear and trouble of soul. I have
been favoured to recover from this in a great measure,
and I wish to remember that I then felt " the whole busi-
ness of life is to be prepared for death." But I have again
and again grown careless since that monition of the un-
certainty of my continuance here. How alarming it is
to find how soon I can compose myself to rest again when
health seems returning! I think I do feel with gratitude
that it is good for me that I have again been afflicted, and
as though I could more steadily and certainly behold the
merciful dealings of my Heavenly Father in permitting

it to be so ; and may I not believe that all which I have
borne has been altogether needful ? I have been called to
suffer deeply from the loss of my dear sister, I have been
made to feel the world only like a dreary desert, and have
seen its loveliness once more fade and depart. Yes, there
are hearts, and mine is one of them, which will not let the
world go (they hold it too closely) ; but if in pity its
charms are taken from them, and the heart is left to
bleed, then (and it seems not till then) they seek for something to heal the wound ; they pant for peace and for a
refuge that will not fail them. Oh, how thankful ought
I to be that thus *I* have been dealt with and borne with,
and I feel now the dawning of a hope that from this time
I may " prefer Jerusalem above my chief joy." Dear
Martha and I seem now like a garden enclosed, kept from
the many enjoyments which while in health I loved too
well—from those things which were becoming to me
fearful temptations, swallowing up the little seeds of
good. Oh, we must regard ourselves as peculiarly
favoured, peculiarly watched over and guarded. But in
whatever state or station we may be the enemy is at work,
and I find (as dear sister S. expressed) at such times he is
very busy in leading us to fill up our time in too trifling
a way. When we lose a friend, others are kindly sympa-
thizing ; they endeavour to cheer us by lively conversation—they wish to read to us, and try all arts to amuse
and to divert us from the mournful theme. Thus it is
also when they suppose we are low from indisposition,
and it requires great care not to allow our minds to be
too content and comfortable with their endeavours to
make the time pass less heavily. But while we get to be
interested in this way, the mind is, as it were, *blocked* up
with trifling thoughts ; the enemy, if there is not a watch,
will prevent, if possible, the operation of the means appointed to purify and cleanse. Ah ! it is a nice thing to

be *rightly* and thoroughly exercised·by afflictive dispensations—to yield our hearts without reserve to the Refiner's fire; to be willing to endure the whole process; to sink down under the Divine hand, desiring that every particle of all that is opposed to His power should be subdued. Hitherto I have been too soon ensnared by *alleviations*, and have not bowed entirely and humbly to every stroke; but I now begin to see how greatly I have erred, and to desire—through Divine assistance fervently to desire—that the whole of the design in thus afflicting us may be accomplished; fully wrought out. It seems to me strange that I should be now putting my desires on paper, after having felt as if I should not do so again, seeing how they are brought to light when the writer is more; but I feel that if I should live longer than I sometimes think is probable, I should wish to refer to the record of these memorable visitations, made when I thought perhaps death was near; and, if in a time of carelessness, it may arouse me to more serious thoughtfulness, it will be of some use. I find no tie so strong in this life as dear Martha; when she is very ill I think I may be the only sorrowing sister. But oh, I have found how wonderfully hard things have been made easy, although the struggles of nature are sometimes violent; how hard to bear is that deep, that heartfelt loneliness, that ' quietness of grief,' that feeling of dull heavy desolation, which the void in our circle has produced.

> ' But words are powerless to reveal
> The grief, the joy, I sometimes feel.'

"12 month, 10, 1830, (the day after my precious M's removal) W. Impey called, when taking leave he said, 'Remember dear Lucy that the foundation of God standeth sure, having this seal, the Lord knoweth them that are his;' and whatever trials and conflicts thou mayst have to pass through, I believe His everlasting arm will be underneath; there is an unfailing refuge for all those who are endeavouring to place their trust and confidence in Him, and I fully believe thou wilt find this to be the case."

" 12th month, 15. The dear remains were laid in the dust. Oh, to feel thankful enough for the favours of that day! Dear M. King staid with me, and after sitting some time, under the influence of a precious calm, she said affectionately, ' What can be a greater proof of the dear creature being safely gathered than this holy calm? Thou finds it wonderfully to hush the feelings of nature!' Yes, in great compassion it was permitted so to do, for the billows of affliction were not suffered to overwhelm. After meeting, dear mother sat with us, and it was a precious time. She desired that gratitude might be felt towards Him who has so wonderfully and so mercifully supported us through the whole of this affliction; that we might endure every turning of the Lord's hand upon us, and keep the word of His patience when He may see meet that we should go many days fasting, &c.

" I must acknowledge that I have experienced unspeakable consolation at a time when nature unassisted must have sunk beneath the trial of losing such a loving sister, such a sweet kindred heart; nothing in life can repair the loss, but oh! may I seek a nearer acquaintance with my Heavenly Father. May I be willing to resign these earthly treasures, that He may be more than ever my God, my guide and preserver. To reflect on her blissful lot pours into my heart such comfort, that I may well be able to rejoice for her. Sweet, happy one, how thou art and wilt for ever be, praising Him whom thou truly loved! but feeling is now at too low an ebb profitably to commit much to paper, yet I was not comfortable that the day should pass quite unnoticed.

" 12th month, 28th.   Oh, the comfort it is to feel that
though separated from my precious Martha we are not
disunited; I do not feel as if she had entirely left me.
Were I more heavenly minded should I not know more
of the precious fellowship which exists between the Glori-
fied in Heaven and the faithful upon earth.   Oh! my
sweet dear, how have my sighs been hushed when I have
been enabled to see that thou art far from every thing
that can distress thee, that after a long struggle with the
trials of time thou art a partaker of that rest which is
inconceivably glorious.   I cannot wish thee back again;
no! I love thee too much for that, but I long to be prepared to become an inhabitant of the same city.   Oh, to
bow under every dispensation, that so the will of our
Heavenly Father may be entirely done; that I may be
mercifully fitted by the same Love and Power to unite
with those dear to me in celebrating that mercy which has
done so much to redeem a world lying in wickedness.

" First day, 12 month 26, 1830.   Joseph Knight addressed me, and I wish to preserve the substance of his
communication in this way.   He said that when he had
thought of me, as well as at the present time, he had been
led to believe that the Lord would carry on the work, the
great work which he designs concerning me, if I am
bound unto Him in a perpetual covenant; that He will
then condescend to preserve me, to lead about and instruct me, and keep me as the apple of his eye; that He
will uphold me, and never leave nor forsake me, as I am
faithful unto Him who is calling me to glory and virtue,
and that I should be enabled to acknowledge that the
Lord spreadeth a table in the wilderness, &c."

" 1 month, 1st, 1830.   Last night I lay and listened
to the bells ' ringing the old year out and the new year
in; ' it seemed a strange way of observing such a circum-
stance—strange to rejoice because *time* has so quickly

flown; and yet I felt I had reason to rejoice for my two
dear sisters, that they had done with time and all its
trials; that they are happy and eternally at rest. I am
indeed left very solitary; but at the time I seemed more
able to think of my dear ones who are so mercifully
gathered and so safely landed, than to mourn much for
myself; but oh, how feeble I am in every respect! I
have every comfort that I can desire to possess, and my
dear parents are more than ever precious to me. They
are uncertain treasures; but I must not look forward—I
think I do not with anxiety. I know there is one who
ordereth all things right, who ' doeth all things well,' and
with Him, whom I found to be so full of mercy and
compassion, and so ready to afford strength in time of
need, I think I can leave the future."

"2nd month, 1831. Dear Mary Alexander, at the
time of our last Monthly Meeting, expressed her desire
that I might so yield and bend, and give up in the day of
the Lord's power, as that I might be His on His own
terms, that I might tread in that path which she believed
was mercifully opened for me, to take step by step in safe
succession to the ' city which hath foundations, whose
buider and maker God is,' &c. Oh, when shall I resign
all? Even now I flinch from bending my neck to the
yoke—I seem to refuse to give up. I have brought myself into much conflict by wandering from a merciful
Guide and Preserver; I do not love to settle down nnder
the chastening operations of the hand of love. I strive to
get from under it, and seek presumptuously in the world
for that strength and happiness which can only be found
in God, and in simple obedience to Him. Then I am
greatly troubled, and my burden of sorrow makes me
turn again to the ' Friend of the friendless and the
faint.' "

Without exact date. "Yesterday, while the family were at Meeting, my dear Mother was engaged very encouragingly in testimony (in our sitting at home). In the morning, before I was up, and indeed often of late, I felt that my evidences of acceptance in the Divine sight were so very doubtful. I have not been able for a length of time to realize as my own the peculiar privileges of a true Christian. She said very varied and fluctuating as are the states of our minds, yet there is no cause for dismay if there be but an endeavour to make war with our spiritual enemies, not in our own strength, but in the language of one formerly. 'In the name of the Lord I will destroy them.' Although we may experience seasons of probation—of inward conflict and poverty, yet if such be the tenor of our desires, there was, she believed, no cause for discouragement, for our God is greater than our soul's enemies, and though we might not sensibly feel the drawing cords of a Father's love, yet if there was but a longing for preservation, a desire that the meditations of our heart might be acceptable in His sight—if there was but an endeavour to 'stand still,' she believed in the Lord's due and appointed time, we should 'see his salvation.' The next first day was one of peculiar favour; my dear mother was engaged in supplication by the side of my easy chair on my behalf. Oh, I did feel the privilege of having such a parent, and that I should still be condescended to in a time of depression ought to excite heartfelt gratitude."

"2nd month, 15, 1831. The present day is one of some conflict, perhaps it is permitted in order that I may feel more thankful when sensible of the blessing of Divine support. Now, I seem not to know what it is by sweet experience, yet surely I have brought this state of loneliness and fear upon myself. I am now too ready to indulge in the daily gratifications of life, and to rest on its ihnocent enjoyments, which once I could not love to share in, when my ever precious M. was deprived of them. Ah! my only comfort then was in seeking for resignation and support. I am now too apt to forget that it ought still to consist in doing so, and I venture to brave the storm, and to make myself as easy as I can with all the pleasure I can get. Ah! this is little now, and it only wounds and irritates. The recollection of the past, and my present state of weakness, with the excitement produced by seeing my friends, seems, in my lonely condition, almost too much to bear. Resignation is wanting—a patient willingness to suffer. While I am restless and impatient under these trials I shall remain sorrowful and weary of my lot in life. I am carrying my head too high. Oh, to be brought down, patiently to *endure*, for in this there is abundance of happiness."

"2nd month 24. After having recorded how fearful and how full of trouble and dismay I have been, I think I must not omit to pen that when such is my sad condition it is because I have not sought unto my God for relief; it is because I act as if there were 'no God in Israel.' But oh! there is a gracious God, ready to help and to sustain all those who put their whole trust in Him, and who look unto Him with a sincere desire to do so on all occasions, and in every extremity. He is all-sufficient, his gracious support is enough. Without this I 'sink in deep waters.' I wish to bear in mind that when my dear Martha was so very ill, I used to sit beside her couch, feeling (as I believe we did mutually) that our only safety and comfort depended on casting ourselves upon the Lord; we could not flee to any other refuge. This we were mercifully enabled to do, and how from time to time did we receive strength sufficient for our day! She was, I have no doubt, a strength to me; her sweet example, in turning inward, in staying her mind, as far as ability was afforded, upon the Rock of our strength, was indeed calculated to draw her poor sister to seek after the same support. How sweet it is to remember these seasons; we looked to the Lord as our only helper. He was pleased to permit us to put our trust under the shadow of His holy wing. Oh! I would praise Him for his goodness; may I not be ungrateful when I remember the multitude of his tender mercies. I feel that I ought to praise him, and for the last few days He has been pleased to show me again that He is an all-sufficient portion; 'He giveth power to the faint, and to them that have no might He increaseth strength.' But to obtain this how needful is it that *all* my expectation should be from Him. He has in his boundless compassion given me help from trouble, and granted me once more a peaceful calm. I have even been permitted to rejoice, and to thank my dear Saviour for all that He has done for us. He has indeed ' done great things for us,' and with the dear one, who is now no more, I am ready to exclaim, ' Can it be true?' Oh, has he taken her to himself to be with him for ever— to praise Him eternally? Yes, all this He has done. And now can I do less than love and serve Him above all! My cold heart, wilt thou still remain unmoved?"

" 5th month, 1834. I attended Meeting the first time for two years on the 13th of last month, and again three weeks afterwards, and to-day have been again mercifully favoured with a little renewal of confidence in Him who still remains to be the strength of his people—their only safe refuge. May we cleave to Him the Saviour of souls, our only sufficient portion; we cannot 'make our boast' in any other. ' In the Lord Jehovah is everlasting strength.' Oh! He would gather us in His arm, and carry us in his bosom for ever, were we more simply and humbly depending upon Him. Blessed be his name,

He condescends at seasons to manifest his gracious care towards the poorest and the weakest."

" 6th month 3. The weather delightfully warm, and my strength considerably increased; it seems outwardly ' the day of prosperity;' I am less ready, therefore, to ' consider ' than in the day of healthful ' adversity,' yet a blessing will doubtless be dispensed if the fault be not my own ; yes, of equal worth to my soul."

" 6th month 10. This is Colchester Quarterly Meeting day ; I am quite alone. I wish I could make a right use of this privileged time ; there seems a little good near, as if my Heavenly Father had not forgotten me in my loneliness. What a mercy to be permitted to find a little rest after a stormy day of temptation, wherein the depravity of my nature seemed to reign over all that is good. My heart is more prone to wander from the source of all purity than when I had less ability to enjoy earthly things. May preservation be mercifully granted! but it must be more constantly and earnestly sought. May the prayer of my heart be, ' Oh keep my soul and deliver me.' My God is good; He is still ' very pitiful and of tender mercy ': my soul must acknowledge this."

"Garden, 6th month 28th, 1834. Have just been transcribing a few valuable lines written by my Uncle John Brown; they seem peculiarly suitable for myself at the present juncture. The enemy is very busy, striving by various means with a variety of baits to gain me over, tempting me to wander from the safe, the narrow path, which leads to peace and eternal life. I almost think the necessity for watchfulness seems greater than ever. My birthday is just over ! my health remarkably good (for me)"

" 7th, month 18. My dear mother expressed her belief that when we indulge in any gratification which is opposed to the Divine will, we are endangering our souls ; adding ' however strong, however powerful, the temptation may

be, may we remember the query of the dear Redeemer,'
' what shall it profit a man, if he gain the whole world;
and lose his own soul?' May this question often be put to
myself—what will it profit me, if I gain the approving
smile of the world, and lose my own soul? Oh, for a willing renunciation of every sinful, selfish gratification! I
mourn because of their prevalence; they keep me in bond-
age and destroy my peace. But there is a refuge—a healing fountain, to it I trust I sometimes repair with a degree
of faith and hope, and trust I am not mistaken in feeling
that in doing so there is sweet relief."

" 1st month 20th, 1835.   I have to day received a
precious little note from dear J. Knight, who seems to
have had a sense of the danger to which I have been and
still am exposed, for I have felt as if the enemy had been endeavouring to get me to swallow a powerful anodyne, and
he has, I am afraid, succeeded. I have felt its fatally
poisonous effects, conscious that the power of a merciful
God is alone able to counteract them, but am still too
fearless, lukewarm and careless.   May the will of my God
be done."

" 5th month 5th, 1835.   My dearest Mother has been
saying this morning, that she is convinced her lungs are
affected; that she has no wish to stay here, but for the
sake of dear Father and myself."

The increased illness of her dear Mother continued till
the 1st of 8th month following, when she peacefully departed this life, as appears in a memoir printed in 1842.

" 12th month 26. Was mercifully favoured with a
renewal of Divine life, light and faith; the breathing of
my spirit at meeting this morning was, I trust in sincerity,
' thy will be done.' Oh, how pure, how perfect and beautiful appeared the work of God as it is manifested in the
complete redemption of the soul; its operation, how much
to be desired.   My heart was lifted up in contemplating

the sacred employment of redeemed spirits. Its language was ' how do they praise Thee for all that thou hast done for them, for the complete work which thou hast wrought in them.' ' Oh, how precious this realizing faith, desired for me by dear ——. May I be enough thankful for all!"

" 11th month 21st, 1836. For my own instruction I record some of the favours of yesterday. It was our Preparative Meeting. Divine goodness and condescension marked the day as to the exercises of my own soul. Before I rose the words ' All power is given to me in heaven and on earth' (Matthew xxviii, 18) shot comfort though my soul. In the morning meeting how was my spirit engaged to wrestle for the more full operation of the Divine power, upon my own heart, upon the heart especially of poor ——, and many more. I longed for a little encouragement to be handed me and others also. Yes, I did long for the opening of a spring which might wash our hearts, and oh, what cause of thankfulness that my peculiar need seemed so remarkably supplied,—that the longings of my soul were so satisfied."

" Dear W. Impey rose with the words, ' He who has all power in heaven and on earth is able to work *by* means or *without* them according to his own gracious designs, either as it relates to the experience of individuals or in the world,' &c. He said he had been led to remember the smiting of the great image by a stone cut out of the mountain without hands, which so completely brought it to nothing, and expressed his earnest desire that we might be willing to submit to the operations of this mighty power, which would then subdue and break to pieces all which is opposed to the Divine will, and finally establish in our hearts the everlasting kingdom of our Lord and Saviour Jesus Christ. How earnestly he exhorted us to gather to *the power*, to feel after it, to wait in the light, and faithfully occupy with present grace that so step by

step we might advance in the way cast up for the ransomed to walk in, and that we might more clearly see our
spiritual condition in the sight of a heart searching God.
Oh, what cause of thankfulness thus to have been condescended to. I long for more tenderness of spirit as in
former days,—a passive spirit receiving Divine impres-
sions according to his blessed will."

"12th month, 5th, 1836. A sweet return of consolation this morning, after some days of thick darkness, de-
mands a tribute of humble thanksgiving and praise. How
was my spirit depressed by the trials of the day! My dear
father very unwell, appearing to decline;—my precious
sister (in-law) going to leave us;—every thing was gloomy,
and my soul was exceeding sorrowful. Yesterday,
though sadly lifeless, some ' sweet words of cheer ' revived
a little. ' Though he cause grief yet will he have compassion, according to the multitude of his mercies,' solaced
in measure my fainting heart, and there seemed some
quietness in the evening. This morning a degree of
ability was granted to look to the dear Redeemer for his
gracious assistance ; the day began to dawn, and I could
say ' The Sun of Righteousness has arisen with healing
in his wings.' His smiling countenance once more appeared to chase away the clouds, and in Him I felt happy.
What cause there is still to trust in a Friend so faithful,
so merciful, so compassionate. Oh, shall I not trust in
Him for ever ! On coming down to breakfast I found my
dear father much better. This time six years my precious
Martha was proving the love and mercy of her dear Redeemer. How sorely was she tried ! but in his abundant
compassion He at last appeared, and chased away every
fear, then took her in his own kind arms, to be at rest for
ever."

"2nd month 22, 1837. Another precious treasure has
been taken from me—one of my last and dearest. Yet

many and many a time during the illness of my dear and
beloved father, how was I called to trust in Him who ' af-
flicteth not willingly.' As my precious parent became
weaker, still more brightly shone every christian grace ;
such peace was often granted him, that I was enabled to
rejoice. We enjoyed sweet communion together, though
not always through the medium of words ; there were
times when our bosoms were alive to the tenderest emo-
tions—we wept together—we felt that we must part, and
my heart bore the pain of severing love; but again I was
enabled to rejoice in his joy.

"At the commencement of the year he was very ill ;
I was then mercifully supported, and from that time I
would gratefully acknowledge that I have been most tenderly helped. I could not feel at rest any where but in my
dear father's chamber ; there was my home, there was my
dearest earthly treasure, and there we were mercifully permitted to partake together of soul-sustaining nourishment.
It was to me an instructive time. To witness the simple,
lowly confidence, so sweetly evinced; the firm yet humble
hope in Divine mercy, the gratitude for every favour,
spiritual and temporal, was indeed sustaining. A precious
quiet was to be felt at seasons, of which my dear father was
permitted to enjoy much. His words of counsel to many
of his friends, his tender interest in their best welfare, will
I trust be profitably remembered. On the night of the
2nd inst, he was much worse; I was mercifully sustained,
but did not think his end so very near. For two or three
days the cord seemed gently loosening that bound my
heart to his ; it was more and more attracted upwards,
and yet at times its own full flow of love was poured upon
him as I cannot describe. I was very poorly, yet was so
comforted from the words ' Our Father's at the helm,' that
I seemed free from all anxiety. When I went into the
room at five o'clock I found him much worse ; he could

scarcely speak, yet he pulled me down to kiss him, and looked sweetly at me. Nature deeply felt, yet I was not distressed; I was preserved much of the time in quietness and enabled at seasons to lay hold of comfort. During a sweet silence some precious scripture promises were permitted to sustain me. The next morning I felt indeed poor and needy,—for a while I was distressed; it seemed as if my precious father suffered, and I left the room ;—it was too much to bear. A more decided alteration took place in the afternoon, I feared to ask particulars; dear brother and aunts were with him; I found the end was approaching, but was apprehensive the scene was distressing. About seven I was more peaceful, and mentioned my wish to go up stairs; then came the feeling of support—the holy calm I longed for, it was reserved for the needful time. Thus mercifully sustained, I remained a witness of that solemn scene two hours; the feelings of nature were silenced. At nine I found I must leave the room, the difficulty of breathing increasing; the time drew near for the release of the precious spirit. I was feeling sweetly calm, when about ten the joyful tidings were brought me, that every earthly sorrow and every pain was exchanged for ‘ an exceeding and eternal weight of glory,’ through that ‘ mercy ’ to which his dying word bore testimony. I rejoiced ; selfish sorrow hardly gained a place ; and though there were the next day bursts of natural grief, yet my heart overflowed with gratitude and praise. Next morning we sat in silence together; it was a precious season. During the succeeding week nature had many a struggle ; moments there were when I wept bitterly.”

“On the day of the interment I was on the whole much supported ; a sweet quietude was enjoyed while the mourning company stood beside the grave. The meeting was a favoured one, though I was very poor. Sweet was the belief expressed by dear S. Grubb that my precious father had found his everlasting rest in the bosom of his Saviour,— that his spirit was gone up to God. S. G. and J. Allen were largely engaged; the former was led to supplicate fervently that every dispensation might work together for our good,—that we might love our God more and more—love Him entirely."

I cannot describe my feeling on re-entering our little house; sobs and tears only could tell the deep emotion. In the evening I felt a little renewal of strength. The next morning I seemed left 'in darkness, in the deeps,'— in unutterable distress; my lonely situation was felt most desolate. All heavenly consolation was withheld; it was a time of conflict never before experienced. Again a sweet calm ensued; it was like an anchor to my little bark, which has not since been so entirely left to the fury of the elements. No, though amidst much poverty and weakness, again and again my harp has been tuned to praise. The language has often been 'Bless the Lord oh my soul, and all that is within me bless his holy name' Oh, he has mercifully comforted me in my affliction.

"1st month 1st, 1838. Goodness and mercy have ' followed me all the days of my life.' Oh, that gratitude and obedience kept pace with favours dispensed, so far as we poor mortals are enabled to ' render unto the Lord the glory due unto his name.' Surely no little offering should be withheld from Him who in tender compassion has brought me safely through the trials of the last year, granting some renewed ability at the present time to 'praise Him for all that is past, and trust Him for all that's to come.' Oh, to be enabled more frequently in humble faith to adopt the language from experience, ' the Lord is my portion, therefore will I hope in Him."

VERSES

OCCASIONED BY A CHANGE OF RESIDENCE CONSEQUENT ON
THE DECEASE OF HER SURVIVING PARENT IN 1837.

THE FAREWELL.

My own sweet home so fondly loved; that dear con-
    genial shade,
Which many a tear, and many a sigh, ah! dearer
    still hath made,
Where smiles of fond parental love had blessed my
    pilgrim way,
How could I leave without a pang, or how desire
    to stay ?

My Father loved to pass with me the gentle twilight
    hour,
Down in our favourite garden seat, our ivy covered
    bower,
There oft he sat in tranquil hope, its glossy leaves
    among,
While his dear hand would gently train each fresh
    young shoot along.

My Mother's step, and sunny smile, 'twas joy to wel-
    come there,
When in the warmth of summer's sun she sought the
    summer air;
But now they both have wing'd their flight, their joy-
    ous flight to heaven,
And sad and sacred seems the spot to my spirit torn
    and riven.

Yet Oh! my heart, if now it be that thou art called
    to brave,
Life's storm upon a rougher sea, tossed on the rolling
    wave,
Mourn not too fondly o'er the past, but trust that
    Friend above,
Who knows how long each joy may last, and orders
    all in love.

Trust in his wisdom, trust his love, and trust his gra-
    cious care,
Fear only lest thy spirit rove far from the place of
    prayer;
Remember, those so dear on earth, have formed ' a
    glorious band,'
Where all they sought is now possessed in yon far
    happier land.
Their blest Redeemer will be thine, if thou to Him
    dost flee,
And all the riches of their lot shall be conferred on
    thee.

Yet may I hope while trembling still on life's un-
    certain strand,
Safely to cross the rolling flood, and reach the
    ' promised land '?
Yes, if their faith and love be thine, their simple
    lowly trust,
Thou yet may'st hope, life's journey o'er, to mingle
    with the just.

Be willing that thy heart should be the throne of
     One above,
Filled with His power and saving grace, and ever-
     lasting love ;
Offer to Him the sacrifice well-pleasing in His
     sight,
Each sweet enjoyment to His will, and every dear
     delight.

Be willing still to bear the cross on earth a little
     while,
Thy gracious God will strengthen thee through many
     a tear to smile ;
He will support thy sorrowing soul above the opening
     wave,
And prove in grief's o'erwhelming hour, His arm is
     strong to save.

He *will*, for when thy shattered bark by adverse
     winds was driven,
Billows around, and veiled above the smiling face of
     Heaven,
Once more in love He bade thee smile, he led thee to
     the Rock
Which stands unchanged, immoveable, amid the
     billow's shock.

Thy Heavenly Father's tender love, still, still, is left
     to thee ;
This treasure thine, can aught remove thy soul's
     felicity ?
When it is gently showered down upon thy sorrowing
     breast,
Canst thou not own with joy of heart, thou yet art
     truly blest ?

The following extracts from L. J.'s letters of the succeeding years will show the state of her mind, in the
absence of existing private memoranda:—

"*Halstead*, 10 *Month* 16, 1840.

"MY BELOVED FRIEND,

"It seems too long since I heard of thy
welfare, and I wish to thank thee for thy last most affectionate letter; it has comforted me more than once. Oh,
to be enabled to 'lay hold' in stronger faith 'of the hope
set before us!' I trust I have at seasons done so since
writing my last epistle. Divine love has felt once more
precious to my soul, and it is a refreshment to speak
thereof to one who knows its worth—who wonders and
adores—who is longing to know more of its 'length and
breadth and height.' Yet are we permitted, though less
frequently than we desire, to say,

'Sweet the moments, rich in blessing,
  Which before the cross I spend ;
Life and health and peace possessing,
  From the Sinner's dying friend.'

I may do little more now than speak to thee of this Friend ;
just to do this seems precious, but while on the subject,
the starting tear is nearly all the language of the heart
which I can now convey;—to mingle in spirit in silent
adoration may be our most fitting employment. Christ
is precious to us, my dear friend; oh what should we do
without Him, where could we go but to Him? We desire
to be stripped of all self-righteousness—to go empty-
handed to Him, though laden, heavy laden with sin, and
often with sorrow. Those gracious words 'come unto
me—and I will give you rest,' embolden us so to do, and
we are permitted to find this rest in Him, even in the
present life, 'a refuge from the storm.' Oh, if we *kept* near
to Him, how much more should we know of a growing in

grace, and of bringing forth fruit to His praise! This
last sentence should have been written in the singular,
I instead of *we*, yet we both feel our own peculiar
necessities.

"We have cause to be very thankful, my dear friend,
that we are still attended on our pilgrimage by one who is
caring for and watching over us with a jealous eye. Others
little know our dangers—how often the roaring lion is
heard, or the tempting bait is offered. Alas, for the
wanderer, the too easily ensnared! How often am I thus.
I must be honest, and ask thee to remember me in the
fight—in the midst of dangers, but what is worse, as too
ready to yield * * * * How does this cold weather suit
thee, my dear friend? And thy many poor patients; hast
thou still cause to rejoice, and hope that the great work
is progressing amongst them, especially where its
progress has been most anxiously watched? I am one,
I trust, and am grateful for the undeserved and continued
affectionate interest of one who has long been tenderly
loved. I cling so closely, too closely to remaining
treasures, but not enough so to Him, who is, I trust,
still the Beloved of my soul. I am and have been alone
since I wrote, and though often *feeling* so, yet I have been
of late free from great depression; the best of comforters
is in His mercy sometimes near, but I have yet to learn
obedience by the things which I suffer; when will this
be?

"I would be thankful that I am still reaping the
benefit of my late visit to the sea-side, so that what would
be irksome in weaker health is now a suitable employment, though I do not really *act* save in very minor matters.
I shall be very glad to have a favourable report of the
health of your dear circle; never forget, my beloved
friend, that it is to me a real enjoyment to be privileged

to listen to thy joys and cares; perhaps I may soon have this pleasure. Accept my dear love, and believe me

Thy very sincere and affectionate friend,

L. JESUP."

"1 *Month* 8, 1841.

* * * * "I write to thee this morinng, my beloved friend, from a barren wilderness; 'not a flower can I gather that's lovely and sweet.' What must I do, what can I do, more than expose the fact? Yes, many a change has been experienced since I last wrote; blessings have been showered down through anointed servants employed in the vineyard, for which we had cause to be very thankful, but too soon they seem to pass away. Oh, for a right employment of our private hours; how the enemy watches to make these his prey; it matters not what the cause is, if he can employ it to raise obstructions to a near, a very near approach to our Heavenly Father. I can sympathize with thee in all thou suffers in this respect though the cloud arises from a different quarter,

' Whatever passes as a cloud between
The mental eye of faith and things unseen,'

is to be dreaded, and we lament that such hindrances abound when desiring to approach the mercy seat. To ask for blessings on others is a duty, a sweet employ, but we feel that there is a warfare to be maintained, a fight to be fought, a victory to be won, and that great is the need to give all ' diligence to make our calling and election sure.' Surely no one has greater need to meditate on this truth than myself, though my days pass so quietly, and I spend so many hours alone. But how is the enemy of all good on the alert! Think of me, my dear friend, when thou canst, in desire that I may not become his prey. Mayst thou still hold on thy way, 'rejoicing in hope,' finding all thy need abundantly supplied by that God who is faithful to his promise, rich in mercy, and a present helper in the time of need. 'Rejoice in Him' my dear friend, 'glory in his holy name,' 'let the heart of them rejoice that seek Him.' Another year has dawned, accept my best wishes, my beloved F. and my thanks, for thine. My heart has opened a little to thee, like the flower to the sun. With much love believe me ever most truly,

Thy affectionate friend,

L. JESUP."

"*Halstead*, 12 *Month* 3, 1842.

* * * "Shall I, my own friend, once more cover a whole sheet of paper? I should like to brighten half an hour by giving thee a little good news, or by diverting thee from feelings of trying languor. The possibility of contributing an atom to numerous sources of enjoyment (though these, alas! are often rendered less availing by indisposition) emboldens me to hold a little chat in this way. * * * Be assured of my renewed and affectionate sympathy. Oh, all these chastisements will not I think be lost; but they are indeed, 'grievous,' viewed only in regard to the poor body; in the highest sense may we not esteem them 'light afflictions which are but for a moment?' I do think the longing for entire submission is tenderly regarded, and that there are given tokens of love in some seasons of sickness and privation, which a state of health and ease might not afford; here is something for the worn spirit to derive fresh courage from. I remember my dear Mother said to me when I was in grief, expecting to lose her, 'the desire to obtain resignation may of itself, prove a blessing, by drawing us nearer to the source of all good.' Yes my dear friend, think not therefore thou art so very far from obtaining the precious boon. I would not forget, dear——, while writing thus, that it is indeed our calling

to be reaching forth unto those things to which we have not attained; may it ever be our aim to stimulate each other thus to do, and so to seek for Divine food and strength, that we may know ourselves whereof we speak, when thus reviving the language 'Be of good courage;' that there is one, even our Father in Heaven, who loves, and pities, and watches over us, in the tenderest compassion; and whether from storms of temptation, or from the trial of bodily suffering, we seek repose and shelter, may we still be enabled to testify, what a blessed rest is to be found in Him alone. But how long are we learning this; how unwilling to be brought to this acknowledgment! I have, as thou knowest so much cause for mourning and lamentation and fear, that I may well feel unable to 'speak a word to the weary,' but if I know at all where happiness lies, I do long for those I love to drink of it, and I am sure the friend who will soon be reading this, desires this gift for me. A few days ago I felt such a poor little thing, as if thy sympathy would be so soothing;—now I am rather risen again. I did not write, for I only seemed as if any thing was enough almost to crush me. When thus we feel, we ought not to be afraid of really sinking, but with all our load of infirmities seek that very low place, where the most simple and needy are permitted at seasons to revive. I hope I tried to do so,— but yet not enough with my whole heart."

" *Hertford*, 1 *Month* 2, 1845.

" MY VERY DEAR FRIEND,

" Couldst thou *see my heart*, I need not attempt to express what is there, which seems so to belong to thee. It is however, very sweet to have this channel through which to convey so far as we are able,

the love and interest which exists, and which peculiar circumstances sometimes especially re-awaken; sweet to greet
each other *in the love of our Heavenly Father*, which is the
only abiding union; sweet to sympathize in grief or joy,
and oh, how precious to be enabled to 'speak one to
another' of those continued mercies which are shed upon
us, desiring for each other the only true blessing. And
though, my dear friend, I can add nothing to that which
is thy rich possession, I know it is grateful to be assured
that we are *understood*, and it is good to bear testimony,
in however small a degree, to the goodness of our God.
How mercifully is He at seasons renewing our confidence
in Him, in all his dealings with us."

"But if I attempt anything of my own experience, it will
be *just an echo* of those precious lines quoted in thy note,
and the substance of some portions of my letter to my
dear brother; thus my heart dictates. 'How good is our
God,' he gives us to confide in his merciful care—gives
us the desire to take our *all* unto Him, and permits us to
rest in His will—in His wisdom. It is not long that I
have just thus been favoured, dear F.; 'weeds' have
seemed 'wrapped about my head.' 'Oh, that I had
wings like a dove, for then would I fly away and be at
rest,' has been the longing of my heart, and this from a
sense of weariness of flesh and spirit, but a rest even
here is at times the portion of each trusting child, which
makes it willing to bear the day's burden, and chase
away every sad feeling of impatience under it.

"I am truly obliged, my dear friend, for thy kind information, so interesting to me in all points; I know the effort
it often is to write under similar circumstances, and it is
not strange to me to find it is thus with thee. Shall I
put down a portion of scripture which has been precious
to me? 'Wherefore let them that suffer according to the
will of God, commit their souls unto Him as unto a faithful

Creator;' and the other evening my silent musings were upon the bliss above, Rev. vii. 16, 17. My thoughts will be much with you all, in I trust a prayerful desire for the supply of your every need. Our Heavenly Father will prove himself sufficient in each trial of faith, and of that precious one, now a weary pilgrim, you can say, comforting one another with the words—comforting him also—' So shall' he ' ever be with the Lord,' and your hearts turn to the joyous thought of a blessed re-union with the sainted spirit above, so dear to each.

"Farewell, very dear friend, in near affection and sincere sympathy, thine truly."

" *Hertford*, 5 *Month* 19, 1845.

* * * " One who 'knoweth our frame, and remembers that we are dust,' will help us to wade through the tide of natural affection to his own embrace, while the fervent craving of the spirit is to love Him indeed *above all;* and could a separation from our God and Saviour be borne, were the whole world and all our dearest ties in our possession ? I shall hope very much for an improved report of thy loved sisters, and to know that *your* precious traveller has returned in health to his family and friends will be very gratifying ; for the interesting notice of him and of his father I am much obliged. Sweet was thy testimony of the dear friend with whom wast staying, and sweet is thy employ to aid her flight heavenward. I had been dreaming so much of thee the night before I had thy note; so pleasantly too, as if our intercourse was not altogether of this earth, that I was quite pleased to have it so continued. My waking thoughts had also been especially drawn to thee in much love.

" Ever very affectionately, thy friend,

L. J."

The following was enclosed to a highly valued correspondent not of the same religious society as herself :—

"Thoughts on the question, 'Is there not a danger of our imagining true religion is seated in the susceptibilities of our nature,—that we should be passive, and thus we should lose motive ?'

"Is it not to be desired that we *should* be passive—lie passive in the Divine Hand—unresisting—not opposing its operations ? In this state does not the prayer ascend, 'Lord here am I, do with me as.Thou wilt;—teach me to do Thy will, and to glorify Thee by any means thou mayst appoint.' Is there a danger of losing motive when the heart acknowledges 'all my springs are in Thee,' and waits to be set in motion by them? Through indolenc and blindness I consider we lose motive, by not waitin, as we ought for light and power, and thus not receiving in their full extent, those precious truths and holy in-fluences which would actuate to a right performance o' every duty. Thus to be 'thoroughly furnished to all good works,' is indeed a blessing, one which the 'slothful servant' will in vain wish he possessed. Thou dost not ask me plainly, my dear friend, to 'shew thee my faith by my works,' to prove my love by active obedience—but this is what thou wouldst rejoice to see—what thou ar anxiously looking for, that I may not be 'found wanting, that others may not suffer through my neglect, and that our God may not be robbed of His glory. I *love thee fo all this ;* will the time ever come when thou wilt se some such fruit ? Yet does there require a deeper strikin of the root *downward* before fruit can be seen in perfection, and where there is so little of this there must be a cause, and it requires to be searched out. How true thy words, 'snares surround us and arise from within,' an, that 'in the fear of acting in our own strength there is danger of running into the contrary extreme.' Some r

us are too apt to take shelter under this fear. Ah, great is
the need of watchfulness! We must beware of trusting
in imaginary possessions, of trusting in doubtful evidences.
'The susceptibilities of our nature,' although they are not
always untouched by the operation of Divine Power upon
the heart, must not be the rule by which we judge of its existence; the tearful eye may be so because the nerves are weak,
or from constitutional causes, when in another instance the
spirit's exercise may have been great, the heart poured
out in supplication, without visible signs of emotion.
Oh, for more light, more grace, which would set all in
order, within and without! Dost thou not long to add,
'Rather, dear, occupy with present grace, then more will
be imparted?' I wish to feel more and more the deep
import of the parable of the talents."

"P. S. The above was scribbled in the garden, wilt
thou excuse me if I send it as it is in pencil?"

"4 Month 19, 1841.

"HEARTFELT BREATHINGS.

"*One* in the wilderness has proved Thy care,
In the deep solitude—yes, wandering there,
Feeble and worn with sin's oppressive load,
Alone, as if forsaken of her God.

"Treading with tearful eyes her weary way,
Nor brightened by the cheerful light of day;
Mercy, sweet mercy deigned again to bless
That care-worn child in the dark wilderness.

"So may her dear ones rest—
And in sweet confidence apply to Thee,—
After long weariness by wo opprest,
Safe may their dwelling be.

E

" Keep, Lord in safety keep Thy weary fold,
    Watch it in love,—the feeble still uphold,
    Give them to praise Thee for Thy mighty power,
    For all thy mercy in each darker hour."

" 7 Month 25, 1844.

  " ' Leave all to me '—that whispered word
      Oh, I have sometimes gently heard,
      When clouds were hanging over head,
      And the eye marked their course with dread.
      Now, in this hour of threatening pain,
      I seem to hear that word again.

  " And who is this so kindly bears
      The weight of all our griefs and cares?
      The faithful, true, and tender friend,
      ' Our Father,' before whom we bend,
      Though often with a trembling knee,—
      Yet then to hear, ' Leave all to me.'

  " Full well its power to soothe we know,
      While tears the while are made to flow.
      Yet shall we calmly thus confide,
      If rougher seas our vessels ride?
      Oh, doubt not! meekly bend the knee,
      And list again, " Leave all to me."

"7 Month 2, 1845. The language of my heart is
O Lord, Thou art good and gracious, unutterably good,
kind, merciful, tender, mindful of thy drooping, fearing,
and oft wandering ones, who yet at times breathe fervently
for and more constantly desire a closer union with Thee
the source of all good. I think during meeting time
this morning, a hungering, panting spirit was mine, and

in deep poverty I desired that I might be helped, quickened and strengthened. I found when my brother and aunt returned, that gospel messengers had been sent to this meeting (Hertford), and I felt depressed; but these friends, R. F. and J. Foster, have been taking tea with us, and they were led encouragingly to express their belief that the gathering arm of Divine love was around us. * * Surely I may remember the declaration, ' The needy shall not always be forgotten, the expectation of the poor shall not perish for ever.' In tender mercy a piece of bread has been given me in the time of need, and shall I not remember this with gratitude?"

" 2nd Month 17, 1846. Yet once more would I commemorate the merciful remembrance of my Heavenly Father, who has again enabled me to take hold of a few precious promises which surely He hath given for the hour of need, first through dear ——— in a little note, and then by his devoted handmaid S. S., for my help and revival both at home and in meeting. Truly precious were her words at parting, ' Hope on, hope ever, that must be thy motto, I think.' Sweet indeed these words."

" 4 Month 19.

" True to Thy promise, O my faithful God,
   Surely thou hast been with me many a time,
   When but for Thee my spirit would have sunk
   'Neath the deep waters.—Thine upholding love,
   Has been enough in hours of solitude,
   Which else had been most drear. Oh, is it not
   Infinite goodness, thus to fill the waste
   For the lone pilgrim,—thus to cheer, and give
   Fresh courage for the future way."

"5 Month 26. Again alone, experiencing some conflict from depression of spirits. Where my courage now? Where my faith and endurance when not sensibly upheld by the hand of mercy? Yet I think something of a soothing influence has for a little time been granted this evening."

"10 Month 3, 1847. Surely my precious and most merciful Saviour has been with me this morning at meeting, granting some degree of most soothing calm, reminding me of the ' still waters,' and the love of our Heavenly Shepherd.' Could I indeed say ' The Lord is my Shepherd? Precious to my soul is the least evidence of his love! How many are my wanderings and how great my unfaithfulnes, my tender and oft-slighted Heavenly Father only knows ; these are much unrecorded, but now and then I seem unable to withhold thus giving a degree of permanence to an acknowledgment of infinite compassion to one so unworthy.

"This time 18 years much in mind. Dear P.'s interment."

"11 Month 11, 1847. Felt the 19th and 20th chapters of John very precious. A renewed sense, I think, granted, of a Saviour's love. Jesus died to save our souls—yes

> ' Twas to save thee, child, from dying
> That thy blest Redeemer came.'

And now, ' ascended up on high,' ever living, ever watchful, in tender mercy He is graciously visiting our souls, proving himself the same who in years past drew near unto us, enabled us in faith to look believingly unto Him as a Saviour, gave us to trust in Him in the hour of sorrow, and to feel Him to be a sufficient portion—our rock and refuge—His arms of love our resting place. Oh, that my love had kept burning; but how dimly has it flickered on! Mercy alone has kept it from being quite extinguished. Oh, that the flame may become brighter, and steadily burn to the praise of Him who has enkindled it."

" 10 Month 31, 1850. A gospel visit from a dear friend has, I think I may trust, been a help and refreshment to my almost fainting spirit. It has seemed at times as if strength and faith would fail, while bodily infirmity has pressed the spirit down ; the enemy has been at work to frighten and keep me from my only refuge. Last evening we were favoured with a calm, when he expressed the sympathy he had felt with me under my bodily affliction, yet he believed my Heavenly Father had designed it for the health of my soul. ' I have refined thee, but not with silver, I have chosen thee in the furnace of affliction '; believing that as I maintained a deep indwelling with the source of all good, and was engaged to abide the refining process, I should be blessed in it, &c."

" 11 Month 20, 1851. Yesterday a dear friend was led to address me in an encouraging manner, under feelings of sympathy with me. I trust I may be thankful in the hope that it was a little brook opened for my help and refreshment by Him who I think I can believe is still mercifully disposed to preserve and sustain his poor and often faint and weary child. If I would be found growing in grace there must be an abiding endeavour to seek to live more and more upon Him, who is indeed 'the Bread of Life;' to 'receive of his fulness,' to answer every call, if it be but to turn a listening ear to Him. Not heeding these calls brings leanness and poverty; the spirit wanders shorn of strength—is weary, faint, and ready to fail."

" Bath, 4 Month 3, 1853. ' Be still and know that I am God,' passed sweetly through my mind, producing, after much anxiety and tossing, something of a calm. This mercy brought renewed trust and thankfulness ; and more than once since, when looking anxiously forward, the promise ' I will help thee, yea I will uphold thee with the right hand of my righteousness,' has I think been permitted to carry me on safely from one wave to another,

giving at seasons a degree of prayerful dependence upon
our alone merciful and all-sufficient Helper."

"9 Month 11, 1853. At meeting sat in a state of
extreme poverty and weakness, desiring rightly to bear
such a sense of powerlessness and want of help. A friend
revived the words, ' I am come that they might have life,
and that they might have it more abundantly.' He said
the desire had arisen that we might so wait upon the Lord
as to receive of his goodness; of those blessings which He
will mercifully dispense to the soul which is truly hungering and thristing after righteousness, and which desires
to leave all to the care of the un-slumbering Shepherd of
Israel. Such cravings have of late been raised in my poor
heart, and it should indeed be cause of thankfulness. I
seem afresh enabled to hope in that mercy which is so
unmerited and unspeakably precious."

"5th Month 25, 1855. Last seventh day morning I
awoke with these words passing through my mind, ' The
summons is coming, the summons is coming, may I
be prepared to answer it.' They did not leave much, if
any, impression, yet feeling more poorly of late they have
not unfrequently been pondered.

" I went to meeting on first day, and for some time after
sitting down could only rest after the exertion of getting
there. Then was just enabled to ask if but for a few
crumbs of bread which might fall from the Master's table,
and I thought the passage, ' Thou openest thy hand, they
are filled with good, thou satisfiest the desire of every
living thing,' seemed suited to strengthen the little grain
of faith, and that I might receive it as a token for good,—
as an evidence of the compassionate regard of Him who
careth for the sparrows.

" Some prayerful desires have since been raised for
preservation and help, but alas! there has been far less of
steady watchfulness than would have been experienced by

a heart really and constantly devoted to the divine fear ; a careless wandering has much prevailed, nothwithstanding this return of cough, which is, I think, rather serious. I am not much ' exercised thereby' as I should be."

" 6 Month 11. Much to be thankful for; wonderfully better ; at meeting yesterday."

" Dover, 8th month 17, 1856. First-day. It was comforting to set in silence together this afternoon, and with the ability afforded, to make known our wants and weaknesses to the ' Inspirer and Hearer of prayer,'—the alone Helper of the helpless. I trust we felt it good thus to draw nigh to the Rock of our strength,—the Source of all good. I am made very thankful for my dear brother's restoration thus far, after a time of great anxiety and fear, and have craved for resignation under present suffering : yet this has not always been enough earnestly sought. I did and do desire to trust,—to cling to the only Friend who is unchanging.

> ' The gentlest sire, the best of friends,
>   To thee nor loss nor harm intends,' &c.

were sweet words brought to remembrance when full of anxiety."

The subjoined from more recent letters may close these Extracts.

" *Halstead*, 3 *Month* 27, 1851.

" MY DEAR FRIEND,

" I am inclined to write a few lines to tell thee how very glad I was to hear from thee once more. I had missed thy occasional and acceptable, though undeserved communications, and *all but* put pen to paper to give thee a ' greeting.' Yet this I am now-a-days rather slow to do, perhaps to my own loss. I have often remembered thy kindness in allowing me to see that letter from thy friend which informed thee of her being acknowledged as a minister ; it was very interesting. Mayst thou

my dear ——, be favoured to proceed safely in the path
marked out for thee, without undue discouragement; ' help
is laid on One who is mighty.'—One who is also compassionate and most merciful. May we each, according to our
need, receive of his fulness, and advance according to his
will in the class to which we may each belong; both I
hope, in the same school. * *

" Thy desire for me, my dear friend, is sweet that by
every trial of bodily weakness, I may be drawn nearer to
our precious Saviour, Oh, may it be so! Surely, He is very
' precious ' to me; then why am I not more willing to
suffer, more constant in desire to be led aright, remembering that it is ' through much tribulation ' we must ' enter
the Kingdom,' a truth which so often seems to have to be
presented anew.

" I have of late felt a very poor thing as to bodily
strength, and I get *so thin*; I sometimes think, surely I
shall not very long hold on thus; the spirit is ready to
long for its release; the better world looks more and more
desirable.   But then comes the query, why is this? Is it
not the weariness of the flesh, which is longing for rest,
and would it not prove to be so, if the call came forth?
where would then be the ' hope full of immortality ?' * *

" Oh yes, I too find hardly anything so refreshing and
soothing as the sweet air, when mild enough to be enjoyed ;
I think I have been rather better for the last one or two
rides.

Accept much love from
Thy affectionate friend,
L. JESUP."

" *Halstead*, 1 *Month* 27, 1852.

" * * I seem to fear that the clouds will thicken rather
than the contrary,—I have written hoping soon to hear
again. I seem undergoing a course of discipline, and

sometimes as if pressed down under it. Yet I think I feel our merciful Helper near, and some ability to trust in Him, so that the poor mind is not greatly tossed. But I must expect more of this, how needful therefore to endeavour to keep near to our Refuge! I think I must tell thee of a few sweet remarks contained in a letter from——; she says, ' may it be a year of blessing, of strength to do or suffer the will of Jesus;—we need not wish to look forward. It is a great comfort to me often to dwell upon the words ' Your Heavenly Father knoweth that ye have need of all these things;' to *know* our need is with Him to *meet* it,—but in his own time and way; and so for the coming year with all its probable changes and pressing events we ' will trust and not be afraid.' F. knew nothing of our unsettlement; the above is sweet for thee my dear ——, also. Yes, I think I do understand the feelings thou describes; wait a little longer in hope and trust my dear one, and then—Oh then—surely there will be an entrance granted thee into that Kingdom where thy beloved ones dwell, with whom thou shalt for ever unite. Thine may be a ' trembling hope ' still, but it is ' as an anchor to the soul, I do believe."

" 6 Month 1, 1864.

" MY BELOVED FRIEND,

" I must make some addition to my last dismal scrap, assuring thee that my thoughts often visit thee in affection and sympathy—you, I may say. I do believe, however, that having arranged for the best, thou art endeavouring to view the brighter side, and I am sure I would wish to help thee to do so. Oh, how true that ' this not our rest;' we are each taught this, yet how slow is *one* of us to learn; but surely this one lesson even *I* have learned; then alas, there is a stopping short of fully embracing the blessed reality—earnestly striving to secure that which will stand the shock of every wild wave, so as to enable us to say, I am not, I shall not be, ' greatly moved.'

" I do trust thou art at times made to cast thy anxieties upon thy ever faithful Friend. He who has helped, does help, and will eventually help thee, I can believe.

"Is it not very nice to welcome summer at last? I did enjoy the garden yesterday—the first *evening* I have been out."

"2 Month 27, 1855.

" I want to tell thee, my dear friend, that a *current of love* followed thee home; I *almost* told thee so in a little note, which, however, *I did not write.* Thy kind Christian greeting, thou seest was not lost upon me. I felt more than once that I was not with you at the meeting; it may be well that it should be so, and awaken the enquiry why it is I am such a lone one on my pilgrimage. Thou trusts I am not a forsaken one; sometimes I think I can hope so, but there does indeed need a closer clinging to our Heavenly Friend. The enemy is so very busy,—trifles and a wandering mind often depriving me of that strength and refreshment which my solitary allotment might afford if rightly improved. Oh, my dear ——, the manifold conflicts which attend us from infirmities both of flesh and spirit! But was it not so in 'the days of old, the years of ancient time?' And the trusting ones were always delivered. So let us not 'faint when we are rebuked,' but strive to walk more watchfully, and in fresh willingness to suffer, though very humiliating may be our experience."

"11 Month, 1855.
* * * " Sweet to me and just what I so much need, are thy good desires for my help. I am now as

in a mist—nothing clearly discernible of *in* or *externals*; but oh, I could feel how precious was the experience of your dear cousin, who now probably is in possession of *that* of which he had so bright a view." (Alluding to some trials experienced by her friend.) "But I ought not to string together these dismalities—much rather would I help and comfort thee; and if I were rightly exercised for thee, should I not in heart rejoice for all that bows thee as a child, and leads thee near thy God? This is the real blessing, and I do not forget it. I am sure *thou* dost not, although these apparently small trials will have their effect upon a weak frame."

"2 Month, 1856.

* * * "May we be enabled to comfort one another! In all, my dear friend, thou art, I trust, kept from becoming a prey to the rude billows, when they seem ready to overwhelm. Hast thou not thought of us the last few days? Our dear and valued friends left us yesterday; they sat with us after breakfast, just a nice time for me. It was a truly strengthening and consoling season. I would that this shower of gospel love may be as abiding as I believe it is mercifully designed to be."

The three following Extracts are from letters to a junior relative.—

"8 *Month* 29, 1850.

* * * "All, we cannot doubt, has been permitted in tender mercy and loving kindness, and mayst thou, dear love, be enabled to trust in the watchful care of the Heavenly Shepherd, who 'gathers the lambs with his arm, carries them in his bosom,' and comforteth the orphan, even as a mother her child. Oh, how very sweet the thought that the *same light and love* which is the glory of the world above, extends to us, poor mourners here, though in a less degree, and nothing shall be permitted to harm us, if we are 'followers of them who through faith and patience inherit the promises.'

* * * Remember that I know what it is to weep for a precious parent; thy deep and various sorrows I can well understand; but I feel as if I must here advert to that better and availing sympathy which can alone be found sufficient for thy need, and mayst thou be enabled to pour out thy heart into the bosom of Infinite Love."

"2 Month 27, 1855.

* * "I do not forget that this will reach thee on thy birthday. Oh! thou must miss thy precious mother's affectionate greetings. Yet thou hast been so mercifully cared for hitherto that I trust thou wilt be enabled to thank thy God and take fresh courage. Very sweet are the lines

> 'He who hath helped thee hitherto
> Will help thee all thy journey through,
> And give thee daily cause to raise
> Fresh Ebenezers to His praise.---'

Read that sweet piece of W. Allen's whenever thou feels rather flat; it has comforted many a sorrowful spirit."

"5 Month 24, 1855.

After alluding to the attendance of the yearly meeting.

"Thou *dost* prize this privilege, however sad that more real profit is not gained, for such a feeling may at times prevail. Yet do not be discouraged; hold fast that which is good, though it may indeed seem to thyself but as the 'grain of mustard seed;' always give heed to the still small whispers of a Father's love. 'Open the door,' remembering the gracious promise to those who do so (Rev. iii. 20.). Many beside thyself, dear, are sad at heart, because of their unwillingness to resign themselves fully to the love and guidance of Him who yearns to bless and to do us good. But instead of sinking under this consciousness let us resolve, ' I will arise and go to my Father, I must not linger short of his embrace.' It is indeed well to be jealous of ourselves, and a mercy to be convinced of our sins and shortcomings; under these feelings the soul which flies in faith to its compassionate Saviour is in his own time relieved of its burden, and is made to desire to keep very near unto Him—in the way, the narrow way which leads to life. In the words of a young Jewish convert I would say, ' Do let Jesus have all his own will concerning thee.' "

During the earlier part of the year 1857 the subject of this memoir continued in almost her usual state of health, but after a few days of increased indisposition, on 6th month 15th, she felt so ill as to call in a medical man, who pronounced the complaint acute bronchitis, and her state of prostration was such as to alarm him; from this she somewhat improved for about a week, but after the above date was confined to her bed, and gradually declined.

A few of her expressions during this time of weakness follow.

6 Month 23. She wrote on a slate (to avoid the exertion of speaking). " Some days before I was ill, day after day I think, the language ' He shall cover thee with his feathers, and under His wings shalt thou trust' was brought to my mind, and made me to look up—almost to ask why; but in the illness I have been remarkably dead and stupid, yet trusting a little, I hope. "

25. The doctor examined the chest, and found the right lung much impeded in its action. In the evening dear L. enquired what his opinion was, and being told that he did not expect much improvement, some allusion being

also made to ' Like as a father pitieth his children, so the
Lord pitieth them that fear Him,' she wrote, " He has not
been so sensibly near of late; ' unless He hold me fast. I fear
I must, I shall decline, and prove a wreck at last.' Do ask
Him in His great mercy to hold me fast. for I seem as if I
could not get near in prayer, as when I am well."

26. Feeling very faint after changing her position she
said, " Surely any one in my weak state cannot continue
long;" adding that she had been too negligent in spirituals,
but the Saviour was *her* Saviour and *her God*. She wished
not to go without making that acknowledgment.

30. Had passed a poor night, but in the morning
appeared quiet and comfortable, saying " After a storm
comes a calm." Allusion was made to the harbour of
mercy; she replied "Yes, there is nothing but mercy to
trust to:" Part of John xiv. being read, "I hoped that
would be the chapter;" then wrote, " I was musing on my
wonderful position; can it be that Heaven really does
await me? How can it be? Then I think there seemed
like a little settling into a hope that surely so it is, but
still how faint the glow of feeling."

7 Month 5. After hearing John xviii. she said,
" Wonderful love! it has often been the subject of con-
templation in health; I trust it has been the chief theme."

6. On waking from sweet sleep, ' Bless the Lord, O my
soul, and forget not all His benefits."

13. After reading, reference being made to the text
" For we know that if our earthly house of this tabernacle
be dissolved, we have a building of God, a house not made
with hands, eternal in the heavens." " Yes, that is the
great support, ' *For we know*.'"

28. Scripture reading (which she made a point of
having, when able, twice in the day) was succeeded by
lengthened silence, when she said, "I was thinking that
goodness and mercy is near." " The angel of the Lord

encampeth round about them that fear Him, and delivereth them."

31. Much tried with cough, &c , but asked for a little reading; "I should like a Psalm of praise."

8 Month 4. A trying day from the heat and closeness of the weather, but late in the evening expressed thankfulness for many comforts. "Of all sorts"—alluding to the preciousness of a Saviour, "He is all—He is everything—perhaps *I* ought not to say so. When the doctor (yesterday) said I was better, it made me a little anxious lest the time should be much prolonged, but now I can leave it."

25. A trying night was succeded by suffering through the day. In the evening heard Psalm ciii., and lay more quiet. "Whence does this quiet feeling come?" Afterward she said with much feeling, "Can a woman forget her sucking child? Yes, she may forget, yet will I not forget thee."

27. Surprised at her great weakness, but after reading felt inwardly strengthened, and said "That which I have trusted to will not fail."

29. Early in the morning in much pain, "all over," but became more easy, and slept. On awaking, "May I say, 'Jerusalem my happy home?'"

> "Jesus, thy blood and righteousness
> My beauty are, my glorious dress."

30. Heard Psalm cxviii. "His mercy endureth for ever." "Yes, it has endured towards us." In the evening said John x. was very precious to her just before her illness; she thought now she could almost *see* the Saviour. His words, 'I ascend to my Father and your Father, to my God and your God' were comforting.

31. Though very weak, listened to John xvii., which she said was very sweet, thought she had never felt it

sweeter. Speaking of her long experience of debility, she said "I was a wild child, but the dear Saviour mercifully laid hold of me, and gave me faith in him."

9 Month 1. When suffering great oppression of the chest, it was said, "To depart and be with Christ is far better,"—She replied, "Yes, it *must* be far better,' and repeated it.

2. Repeated the two first lines of the following stanza. (somewhat altered.)

> "I think there is prepared
> Unworthy though I be,
> For me a blood bought free reward,
> A golden harp for me."

Later, "I want patience very much, more than you can know." She has taken hardly any nourishment to-day, but though very weak, has been preserved mentally clear.

3. It was remarked that a peaceful quiet was with us. She replied, "I hope it is so." About noon the voice of supplication was raised on account of the dear sufferer by a beloved friend who had been in kind attendance during most of her illness, that in the right time an easy passage might be granted, and soon after six o'clock the prepared spirit was gently released from its afflicted tabernacle.

"BLESSED ARE THE DEAD WHO DIE IN THE LORD."